THE BLACKSMITH AND THE DEVILS

Retold by María Cristina Brusca and Tona Wilson

Illustrated by María Cristina Brusca

Henry Holt and Company

New York

To Beatriz Arágor of the *Pampas News*

Text copyright © 1992 by María Cristina Brusca and Tona Wilson
Illustrations copyright © 1992 by María Cristina Brusca
All rights reserved, including the right to reproduce
this book or portions thereof in any form.
First edition
Published by Henry Holt and Company, Inc.,
115 West 18th Street, New York, New York 10011.
Published simultaneously in Canada by Fitzhenry & Whiteside Ltd.,
91 Granton Drive, Richmond Hill, Ontario L4B 2N5.

Library of Congress Cataloging-in-Publication Data
Brusca, María Cristina.
  The blacksmith and the devils / by María Cristina Brusca and Tona
Wilson; illustrated by María Cristina Brusca.
  Summary: In this Argentine version of a Hispanic folktale, a
blacksmith makes a deal with the devil to extend his youth and good
fortune.
  [1. Folklore—Argentina. 2. Blacksmiths—Folklore.] I. Smith
and the devil. English. II. Wilson, Tona. III. Title.
PZ8.1.B8374B1 1992 398.21'0982—dc20   92-176

ISBN 0-8050-1954-5 (English edition)
10 9 8 7 6 5 4 3 2 1
ISBN 0-8050-2411-5 (Spanish edition)
10 9 8 7 6 5 4 3 2 1

Designed by Anna DiVito

Printed in Mexico

Foreword

After a long day of driving cattle across the pampas, the gauchos sometimes sit out under the stars, telling stories. Stories of their own exploits, or of ghosts they have seen, or stories like this one. This is the tale of Juan Pobreza the blacksmith, known in Argentina as "Miseria," and in Spain as "Pedro de Urdemalas," and all over the Americas by many other names. Like other folktales, this story was not written down for many years but was passed from one person to the next by being told aloud. In the same way a joke or an anecdote changes a little with each retelling, so does a story. People don't remember stories word for word. They like to add a little something of their own, leave out something else, or change the names of the characters or the landscape to fit the place of the telling.

We've based this version on the tale as it was told by the famous Argentine gaucho don Segundo Sombra. Like other retellers, we've changed a few things. We invite you, too, to make the story yours by changing it in any way when you tell it to your friends.

Juan Pobreza the blacksmith lived way out on the pampas of Argentina. His name suited him perfectly, since *pobreza* means "poverty" in Spanish. He'd always been poor, but he'd never turned anyone away for lack of money. All day he worked hard in his shop, often without being paid, and though he was an old man now, he'd never spent a night away from his little village.

But his life was about to change. One hot afternoon when he
was sitting in front of his shop, hoping only for a cool breeze to
come his way, he saw far off in the distance a ragged old gaucho,
leading a mule that seemed to be limping. "Lost its shoe,"
thought Pobreza, and he went into the shop to fire up the forge.

Sure enough, before long the gaucho knocked at the door of the shop and asked the blacksmith if he'd make a new shoe for the mule.

There were only scraps of rusty, useless metal in Juan Pobreza's shop, since he had given away anything good long ago. But as he poked through a pile of junk, hoping to find something that would do for a horseshoe, he suddenly spied a large shiny ring— made of pure silver! He picked it up and put it onto the forge, melted it down, and hammered it into a shoe for the mule.

The old gaucho was very pleased with the shoe, and asked what he owed. But the blacksmith, seeing him to be as poor as he was himself, would not charge the gaucho a penny.

But the stranger insisted. He leaned toward Pobreza and whispered in his ear: "I'm not what I seem to be. I'm really San Pedro, guardian of the gates of heaven. Since you've been so good to me, I'll grant you three wishes—anything you want! But if I were you, I'd wish to go to heaven."

Pobreza looked at the stranger out of the corner of his eye. "This old gaucho must be crazy," he thought, but all he said aloud was, "Sure, sure, three wishes. Let's see...I wish that whoever sits down in my chair can't get up...until *I* say so! That'll keep me from being so lonely," he said with a chuckle.

"Granted," said the old gaucho. "And now for your next wish. And *this* time you'd better wish to go to heaven!"

"Don't you tell *me* what to wish!" snapped Pobreza. "See that fig tree? I wish that anybody who's fool enough to climb that tree can't get down until *I* say so!"

"Oh, all right! Granted!" said the stranger grumpily. "Now this is your last chance, so you'd better not waste it! Wish to go to heaven, I tell you!"

"Shut up, you fat old idiot!" said Pobreza. "I wish that anyone who gets into my tobacco pouch can't get out until *I* say so!"

"Granted," snarled San Pedro, and he got onto his mule and rode away.

As soon as he was alone, Pobreza started thinking. Maybe those wishes had been real, and he had wasted them! "What a fool I've been!" he moaned. "If the devil himself were to walk through my door right this moment, I'd sell him my soul for twenty years of youth and a bag full of gold!"

No sooner had he said these words than an elegant gentleman
with a pointed tail appeared in the doorway.

He introduced himself as Mr. Wetcoals, and offered Pobreza
a contract—twenty years of youth and a bag full of gold, in
exchange for his soul.

Pobreza eagerly signed the paper, and the gentleman vanished,
leaving behind him a strange smell of sulfur.

Pobreza counted his gold and then looked at himself in the
duck puddle. He was young again!

From that day on, his life changed. He invited all the people of
the town to a great fiesta that lasted seven days and seven nights.
There was more to eat and drink at his table than there had been
in the whole town for years. Then he left his guests snoring and
set off to travel around the world.

For the first time in his life, he saw mountains, the ocean, and the big city of Buenos Aires. He rode elephants in India and camels on the banks of the Nile. He spent a night in the tent of a sheik, and another in the palace of an emperor. He hobnobbed with mayors and governors and princes. He fell in love with princesses and they fell in love with him.

The twenty years flew by, and before he knew it, Juan Pobreza
had to return to his old shack. Mr. Wetcoals came to the door,
with the contract rolled up under his arm.

"I'll be ready in a second," said Pobreza. "Take a seat—anywhere."
There was only one chair, and Mr. Wetcoals sat down in it.

When Pobreza returned, neat and clean for his presentation in hell, he found Mr. Wetcoals struggling furiously to get out of the chair. Then Pobreza remembered San Pedro and the three wishes. He roared with laughter. Mr. Wetcoals couldn't get up until Pobreza let him, and Pobreza wouldn't let him until he'd signed *another* contract, giving the blacksmith twenty *more* years of youth and all the gold he wanted.

Pobreza was young again, and he spent another twenty years in the great world, with actors and actresses, kings and queens. He stayed at fancy hotels, ate caviar, and sailed in yachts. He crossed the ocean in a balloon, climbed the Alps, and learned thirty languages. The parties and banquets he gave were the most magnificent in the whole world. But soon those twenty years too were over, and Juan Pobreza returned to his old shack.

This time Mr. Wetcoals didn't come alone. He brought another devil with him. Again Pobreza asked the devils to take a seat and wait for him. But they were determined not to be tricked. "We are *not* sitting," they said.

"Well, then," said Pobreza, "perhaps you'd like to try some of my figs. They're the sweetest and juiciest in the world!" Mr. Wetcoals didn't trust him, but his friend climbed into the tree and started gobbling up all the ripe figs. He smacked his lips and shouted down how good they were. Mr. Wetcoals had a terrible sweet tooth, and finally, forgetting his fears, he too climbed up into the tree.

When Pobreza saw the two devils up in the tree, he howled with laughter. "Are you ready, devils?" he called up to them. But they couldn't get down until Pobreza let them, and he wouldn't let them until they'd signed *another* contract for twenty *more* years of youth and riches.

Once again Pobreza was a young man, and he returned to the life that was now familiar to him. He traveled about the world in his very own airplane, scattering money and jewels as he flew over. But at last those twenty years too came to an end.

Pobreza returned to his old shack, which was crumbling and overrun with weeds. This time not one devil, not two devils, not even three devils, but all the devils in hell, with Lucifer himself in the lead, were waiting at his door.

"Are you looking for me?" he asked.

"We certainly are!" said Lucifer.

"Well, I've never seen you before, sir," said the blacksmith, "and I've certainly never signed a contract with you."

"So what?" roared Lucifer. "You're coming with me, because *I* am the KING OF HELL!"

"Am I supposed to believe that?" Pobreza laughed. "If you were *really* the king of hell, you could get that whole crowd of devils inside you and turn yourself into a little tiny ant! But you're not, so you can't!"

Lucifer was so bad, and so proud, and so angry that he didn't
stop to think it might be a trick. He shouted a magic spell, and
then there was nothing left where the devils had been but a little
tiny ant.

Not wasting a second, Pobreza picked up the ant and slipped it into his tobacco pouch. Then he put the pouch onto the anvil and began to hammer at it with all his might. He hammered and hammered, until his shirt was soaked with sweat.

Every morning he did the same thing—he put the tobacco pouch onto the anvil and gave it a good pounding. And with all the devils shut up in Pobreza's tobacco pouch, things got a lot better on the pampas.

Nobody got sick anymore, and there were no more arguments. Dogs stopped chasing cats. Horses didn't throw their riders, and foxes didn't steal chickens, nor people their neighbors' sheep. And at the general store, even the knife fights stopped. The gauchos, and everybody else on the pampas—even the doctors and lawyers and policemen—lived an easier life.

But not everyone was happy....

A few greedy people, who had gotten rich from other people's troubles, were not pleased. They had a meeting to see what could be done. A doctor complained that nobody needed medicine anymore, and a policeman said that without crime, he was going to starve.

They had heard a rumor that Juan Pobreza, the ancient blacksmith, was keeping all the devils in his tobacco pouch. So before long a delegation of greedy people appeared at the door of his shop.

"We order you to let those devils out of your tobacco pouch! We know they're in there!" said the mayor, who was the spokesman for the delegation.

Pobreza was very tired, and he could think of no more tricks, so he said he would let the devils go. But before he did, he gave them one last pounding. Then he opened the pouch and told Lucifer he could go.

Out limped the little ant. As soon as it was out of the pouch, it turned back into Lucifer, and out of Lucifer's body burst all the other devils. And away they all ran, screaming and howling.

Juan Pobreza had lived a very long time, and had done just about everything he could possibly want to do. He was tired of life. He lay down on his bed. He didn't eat or drink anything, and finally he died.

Leaving his body behind, he went up to heaven and knocked on the gate.

When San Pedro came to open it, Pobreza's heart sank. There was no question now—the old gaucho whose mule he'd shoed was indeed the guardian of the gates of heaven. Pobreza hung his head, hoping not to be recognized, but it was no use.

"You had your chance, but you didn't listen to me," said San Pedro. "And what's worse, you called me a fat old idiot!" He slammed the gate in the blacksmith's face.

So Pobreza turned around sadly and went back down to earth,
and then on down the long, steep staircase that leads to hell.

It just happened to be Mr. Wetcoals's turn to meet the
newcomer at the gate. When he saw who it was, he let out a
frightened squawk and ran to warn the rest of the devils.

They gathered behind the gate to stare—from a safe distance—at the man who'd kept them in a tobacco pouch and pounded them every morning. They didn't want to have *him* in hell!

Pobreza pleaded with them. "Please, devils! Let me in!" he called. "I'll never pound you again! I promise!" But they just hissed at him and told him to leave them alone.

At last he turned around and climbed wearily back up the long, steep staircase.

Since neither heaven nor hell would have him, Pobreza still wanders the earth. True to his name, he no longer visits the kings and princesses who were once his friends. But out on the pampas, when there's no bread in the house, or no money for food, or no metal for horseshoes, people still say that it's because of Juan Pobreza the blacksmith, back to haunt them.